CW00969671

The *Bendy* Tree

written by Grace Josephine
illustrated by Hristina Mazneska

Written by Grace Josephine
Illustrated by Hristina Mazneska
Graphic Design by Hristina Mazneska
December, 2023

ISBN 978-0-6488597-3-4

For Alba and Harquin

I extend my heartfelt gratitude to the
immensely talented illustrator of
"The Bendy Tree," Hristina Mazneska.
Thank you for bringing the story to life.

In the enchanted forest of Spiritwood,
Were the oldest trees that have ever stood.

The most striking trees to have ever been seen,
Tall and glowing and emerald green.

But after living in the forest for so long,
They became hardened to life, stiff and strong.

Right in the middle of Spiritwood,
Was a Bendy little tree who was misunderstood.

The big brave trees stood stiff and proud,
They'd mock poor Bendy and laugh out loud.

"Look at his bark, no strength at all,"
"One gust of wind and we'll watch him fall!"

"Oh dear, my boy, you'll absolutely never,"
"Make it through the ghastly weather."

Word in the forest spread far and wide,
That a deadly storm was due to arrive.

"It'll be here by Wednesday," said the tallest tree,
With her branch above her eyes, gazing out to sea.

The storm grumbled from the distance,
With clear aggression and persistence.

Yet over the water, the moon shone bright,
Sheathing the sea with sparkles of light.

As the blazing, scary storm got near,
The trees trembled, shivered, and shook in fear.

The wind howled, and the thunder roared,
Lightning flashed, and the heavens poured.

"Stand stiff and rigid, my fellow trees, it's the wind versus us,"
"Clench and tense, stay strong and tough."

The big stiff trees let out screams and moans,
"Oh, please, scary storm, won't you leave us alone?!"

Their wood cracked with every gust,
"If this carries on, we will be nothing but dust!"

Yet beneath all this madness was a rather strange sight,
It was Bendy the tree, squealing with delight.

In rhythm with the wind, he soared and swooped,
Round and round, he looped and looped.

Not a splinter in sight, nor a twig out of place,
Free as a bird, and a big smile on his face.

"How did you do that?" asked the big stiff trees,
"You made it through with so much ease."

Bendy smiled and gracefully bowed,
Now it was he who was strong and proud.

"When storms and change knock on our door,"
"We must become bendier than ever before."

"Ride with the wind and go with the flow,"
"Adapt and be flexible, and there you shall grow."

Grace Josephine is a children's author with a focus on rhyming picture books that carry a profound philosophical twist. She is dedicated to sharing vibrant stories with concealed meanings, striving to enrich children's lives and shape their perspectives.

Her other publications include the enchanting "Crusty the Orange" and the thought-provoking "Lou the Lost Witch".

Originally from the United Kingdom, Grace made a 'sea change' to Australia in 2014 to embrace the coastal lifestyle. When she's not writing books, Grace enjoys spending time in nature and travelling - both of which are wonderful sources of creative inspiration for her.

Hristina Mazneska is a visual artist, published illustrator and a graphic designer from North Macedonia. She graduated from the Faculty of Fine Arts of the “Ss.Cyril and Methodius” University in Skopje in 2018. She is currently a freelance artist focusing on illustrating children’s books and video games. She can turn every project into a magical illustrated wonderland!

Hristina has experience in the art and animation industry, she is passionate about everything that sparks her imagination, and takes her on a walk to a whole different universe. Every project is special for her. The most recent books she has worked on are “Mother Earth why are you crying?”, “Before It’s Too Late”, “Superhero Identity: Your Quest To Discovering Your Superpowers and Forming an Unstoppable You” and “Crusty the Orange”. She’s exhibited her artwork in numerous galleries in her home country and abroad.